A Beginning-to-Read Book

What's in My Pocket, Dear Dragon?

by Margaret Hillert
Illustrated by David Schimmell

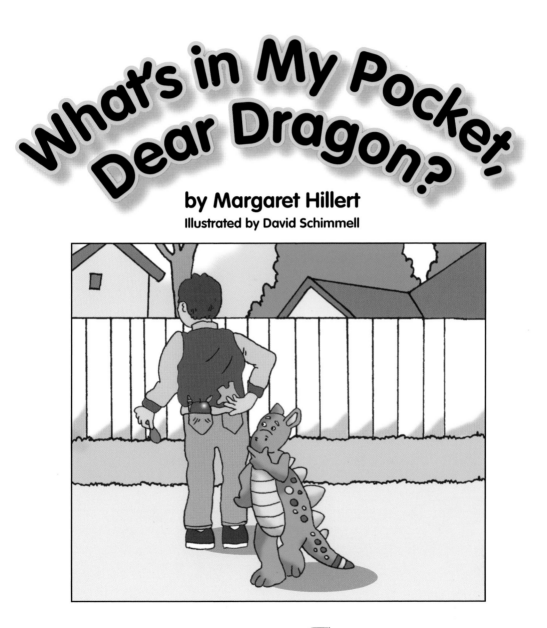

NORWOOD HOUSE PRESS

DEAR CAREGIVER,

The *Beginning-to-Read* series is comprised of carefully written books that extend the collection of classic readers you may remember from your own childhood. Each book features text comprised of common sight words to provide your child ample practice reading the words that appear most frequently in written text. The many additional details in the pictures enhance the story and offer the opportunity for you to help your child expand oral language and develop comprehension.

Begin by reading the story to your child, followed by letting him or her read familiar words and soon your child will be able to read the story independently. At each step of the way, be sure to praise your reader's efforts to build his or her confidence as an independent reader. Discuss the pictures and encourage your child to make connections between the story and his or her own life. At the end of the story, you will find reading activities and a word list that will help your child practice and strengthen beginning reading skills.

Above all, the most important part of the reading experience is to have fun and enjoy it!

Shannon Cannon

Shannon Cannon, Ph.D.,
Literacy Consultant

Norwood House Press • P.O. Box 316598 • Chicago, Illinois 60631
For more information about Norwood House Press please visit our website at
www.norwoodhousepress.com or call 866-565-2900.

Text copyright ©2014 by Margaret Hillert. Illustrations and cover design copyright ©2014 by Norwood House Press, Inc. All rights reserved. No part of this book may be reproduced or utilized in any form or by any means without written permission from the publisher.

LIBRARY OF CONGRESS CATALOGING-IN-PUBLICATION DATA

    Hillert, Margaret.
      What's in my pocket, dear dragon? / by Margaret Hillert ; illustrated by David Schimmell.
         pages cm. -- (A beginning-to-read book)
      Summary: "A boy and his pet dragon learn about sizes and colors as they put items in and take items out of different pockets. This title includes reading activities and a word list"-- Provided by publisher.
      ISBN 978-1-59953-579-1 (library edition : alk. paper)
      ISBN 978-1-60357-434-1 (ebook)
    [1. Pockets--Fiction. 2. Color--Fiction. 3. Size--Fiction. 4. Dragons--Fiction.] I. Schimmell, David, illustrator. II. Title. III. Title: What is in my pocket, dear dragon?
    PZ7.H558We 2013
    [E]--dc23

                        2012043564

Hardcover ISBN: 978-1-59953-579-1   Paperback ISBN: 978-1-60357-415-0

Manufactured in the United States of America in North Mankato, Minnesota.
308R—082017

I have pockets, Dear Dragon.
Pockets are good to have.
You do not have pockets.

Guess what is in this pocket,
Dear Dragon.
Can you guess what's in my pocket?

I'll help you.
It is a black marble.
I play a game with it.

Here.
I'll show you.

And I have this.
See what I can do with it.

Oh, oh.
There it goes.
Look at it go.

Here is something to eat.
Do you want some?
It is good.

I have two pockets.
What is in this one?
Guess. Guess.

Oh, my.
It is a blue car.
I like to play with it.
But, you have to do this first.

Go little car, go.
Run here. Run there.

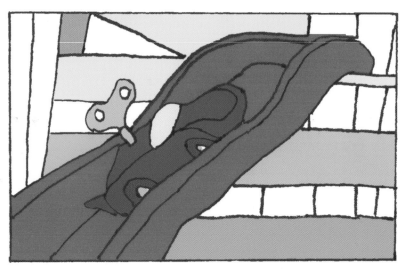

Run up.

Run down.

Oh, no.
Now it can not go.

Now, look what I have here.
I can make something with it.

Let's go into the house.

Put this here.

Look at this.
This was in my pocket, too.
I'll put it away in here.

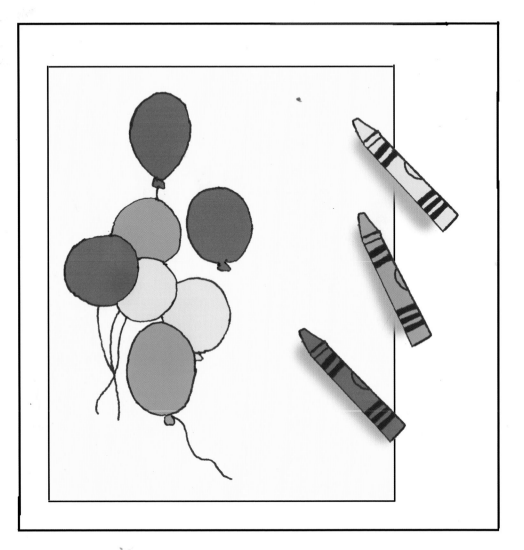

I have some crayons, too.
One is red. One is yellow.
One is green. Crayons are fun.

Mother, Mother.
Can you make a pocket for Dragon?

Well, let me see.
I think I have something.

Will this do?
Dragon, come see this.
It looks like a big pocket.

That is good.
We can put things in.

We can take things out.

Here you are with me.
And here I am with you.
We are good friends, Dear Dragon.

READING REINFORCEMENT

The following activities support the findings of the National Reading Panel that determined the most effective components for reading instruction are: Phonemic Awareness, Phonics, Vocabulary, Fluency, and Text Comprehension.

Phonemic Awareness: The /p/ sound

Oddity Task: Say the /**p**/ sound for your child. Say the following words aloud. Ask your child to say the words that do not end with the /**p**/ sound in the following word groups:

pat, tap, mat	park, map, pack	set, pet, step
peach, reach, sleep	met, pet, up	spot, top, ten
seat, pea, keep	mark, pop, speck	sheep, day, page

Phonics: The letter Pp

1. Demonstrate how to form the letters **P** and **p** for your child.

2. Have your child practice writing **P** and **p** at least three times each.

3. Ask your child to point to the words in the book that start with the letter **p**.

4. Write down the following words and ask your child to circle the letter **p** in each word:

play	help	pretty	puppy	pocket
jump	put	skip	nap	happy
peep	pan	pepper	stamp	purple

Vocabulary: Adjectives

1. Explain to your child that words that describe something are called adjectives.

2. Say the following nouns and ask your child to name an adjective that might be used to describe it (possible answers in parentheses):

   car (fast)   flower (pretty)   apple (juicy)

   marble (round)   coin (shiny)   sun (bright)

   dog (soft)   crayon (little)   ice (cold)

3. Write the nouns on separate pieces of paper.

4. Randomly place the pieces of paper on a flat surface. Read each noun aloud to your child. Ask your child to point to the correct word.

5. Encourage your child to think of other adjectives that can describe each noun.

Fluency: Shared Reading

1. Reread the story to your child at least two more times while your child tracks the print by running a finger under the words as they are read. Ask your child to read the words he or she knows with you.

2. Reread the story taking turns, alternating readers between sentences or pages.

Text Comprehension: Discussion Time

1. Ask your child to retell the sequence of events in the story.

2. To check comprehension, ask your child the following questions:

   • What objects does the boy take out of his pockets?

   • What does the boy do with the balloon?

   • What does Dear Dragon get for a pocket?

   • What is in Dear Dragon's bag?

   • What do you have in your pockets?

WORD LIST

***What's in My Pocket, Dear Dragon?* uses the 85 words listed below.**

The **10** words bolded below serve as an introduction to new vocabulary, while the other 75 are pre-primer. You may wish to write the words on index cards and use them to help your child build automatic word recognition. Regular practice with these words will enhance your child's fluency in reading connected text.

a	first	let	red	want
am	for	let's	run	was
and	friends	like		we
are	fun	little	see	**well**
at		look(s)	**show**	what
away	**game**		some	what's
	go	make	something	will
big	goes	**marble**		with
black	good	me	take	
blue	green	mother	that	yellow
but	**guess**	my	the	you
			there	
can	have	no	things	
car	help	not	**think**	
come	here	now	this	
crayons	house		to	
		oh	too	
dear	I	one	two	
do	I'll	out		
down	in		up	
dragon	into	play		
	is	**pocket(s)**		
eat	it	**put**		

ABOUT THE AUTHOR Margaret Hillert has helped millions of children all over the world learn to read independently. She was a first grade teacher for 34 years and during that time started writing books that her students could both gain confidence in reading and enjoy. She wrote well over 100 books for children just learning to read. As a child, she enjoyed writing poetry and continued her poetic writings as an adult for both children and adults.

Photograph by Glenna Washburn

ABOUT THE ILLUSTRATOR David Schimmell served as a professional firefighter for 23 years before hanging up his boots and helmet to devote himself to working as an illustrator of children's books. David has happily created illustrations for the New Dear Dragon books as well as other artwork for educational and retail book projects. Born and raised in Evansville, Indiana, he lives there today with his wife and family.